All I Want for My Birthday

by Katie Collins

Illustrations by Miruna Craciun

PINK FROG BOOKS

OREM, UTAH, UNITED STATES

For my mom,
who deserves
a great birthday!

Please provide an honest review of this book.

Let Katie know what you did
or did not like about her book.

All I Want for My Birthday

Copyright © 2020 Katie Collins

Illustrations copyright © 2020 Miruna Craciun

All rights reserved. No part of this publication may be reproduced, distributed, or transmitted in any form or by any means, including photocopying, recording, or other electronic or mechanical methods, without prior written permission of the publisher.

For permission requests, write to the publisher at:
permissions@PinkFrogBooks.com

ISBN: 9798690838805

Second Printing, 2020.

Published by Pink Frog Books
www.PinkFrogBooks.com

You asked me what
I wanted for my birthday.

At the time I was
distracted, so I answered
"A well trained dog or dinosaur."

The next day, while we were playing
with your farm animals,
You asked again.

Right then, I was feeling silly.

So I answered
"A pig, a cow or a sheep."

I could ask for
a lion,
a giraffe,
a penguin,
or even...
an entire zoo!

Once, while you were practicing your drums, I thought how much I would rather have a new piano.

When we missed dinner and the play,
I really wanted a new car.

I could ask for
a sewing machine
or a brand new couch!

The day that you
were playing pirate
with your bear,

I said that we needed
a new house.

On Saturday,
when I woke up,
I remembered that
it was my birthday.

1	2	3	4	5	6	7
8	9	10	11 Drum Lessons Play	12	13	14 Mom's Birthday
15	16 Car	17	18	19	20	21
22	23	24	25	26	27	28

I walked into the living room,
and what a surprise!

You were sitting on the floor
with the most wonderful gifts!

A sheep, a pig and a cow
on our own farm.

A dog and a dinosaur,
both well trained!

A brand new house
and a, very small, new car!

YOU!

Katie hopes that you enjoyed her story.

She asks that you provide an honest review of her book
on Amazon.com or your favorite reader's website.
Let her know what you did or did not like about her book.

We would like to offer you a free coloring book.

To download, go to
http://bit.ly/alliwant-coloringbook

To learn more about our books
or to sign up for our newsletter visit
www.PinkFrogBooks.com

About the author

Ten-year-old Katie Collins has always been creative. Growing up with her family in Utah, she has enjoyed creating board and card games, drawing, telling stories, playing with friends and writing code in Scratch. One of Katie's favorite activities is to read, whether the book is audio, digital or print, she loves them all! Katie's favorite book series is Erin Hunter's Warrior series. Early in 2020, Katie began pursuing a dream of becoming a successful author. She is excited that she was able to contribute all of the boys drawings at the end of this book. This is her first book with many more to come.

About the illustrator

Miruna-Oana Craciun, also known as Miruniskaya, is a Romanian children's book illustrator & author based in the UK. Majoring in Graphic Communication & Illustration, she decided to transform her passion for illustrating into a full-time job. You can follow her on Instagram (**@miruniskaya**) or view some of her other work at: **https://www.miruniskaya.com**

Printed in Great Britain
by Amazon

82763016R00018